Santa Mouse

This
book belongs to
Santa Mouse

Santa Mouse

by Michael Brown

Illustrated by Elfrieda DeWitt

Library of Congress Catalog Card Number: AC 66-10903
ISBN: 0-448-04213-4

1982 PRINTING

GROSSET & DUNLAP · Publishers · NEW YORK

Once there was a little mouse
Who didn't have a name.

He lived in a great big house, this mouse,
The only mouse in the whole, wide house.

He used to play a game.

He'd daydream
he had playmates

Who were friendly
as could be.

The boys

would all play cowboys

Or be Eskimos

The little girls
would bring their dolls

And dress up
and have tea.

Or Spanish,

But when he'd try
    to touch them,

Now, through the year,
    this little mouse

Like a bubble,
    they would vanish.

Had saved one
    special thing:

A piece of cheese!

The kind that makes an angel want to sing.

On Christmas Eve, he brushed his teeth,

And as he washed his paws,

He thought, "My goodness, no one gives
A gift to Santa Claus!"

He ran to get his pretty cheese,
And after he had found it,

The paper from some chewing gum
He quickly wrapped around it.

And then he climbed in bed and dreamed

That he was lifted high.

He woke to find that he was looking
Right in Santa's eye!

"I thank you for my gift,"
said Santa.

"Tell me, what's your name?"

"I haven't any," said the mouse.

"You haven't? That's a shame!

"You know, I need a helper
As I travel house to house,
And I shall give a name to you:

I'll call you Santa Mouse.

"So here's your beard,

and here's your suit,

And here's each shiny,

tiny

boot.

"You mustn't sneeze, and don't you cough.

Just put them on, and we'll be off!"

Then over all the rooftops,
On a journey with no end,
Away they went together,
Santa with his tiny friend.

And so, this Christmas, if you please,
Beneath the tree that's in your house,

Why don't you leave
a piece of cheese?

You know who'll thank you?

Santa
Mouse!

This
book belongs to
Santa Mouse